## This book belongs to:

Mr. Nagra

Berryland
Books

Edited by Claire Black
Illustrated by Eric Kincaid

Published by Berryland Books
www.berrylandbooks.com

First published in 2004
Copyright © Berryland Books 2004

ISBN 1-84577-072-2
Printed in India

# Cinderella

# Reading should always be FUN!

Reading is one of the most important skills your child will learn. It's an exciting challenge that you can enjoy together.

*Treasured Tales* is a collection of stories that has been carefully written for young readers.

Here are some useful points to help you teach your child to read.

Try to set aside a regular quiet time for reading at least three times a week.

Choose a time of the day when your child is not too tired.

Plan to spend approximately 15 minutes on each session.

Select the book together and spend the first few minutes talking about the title and cover picture.

Spend the next ten minutes listening and encouraging your child to read.

Always allow your child to look at and use the pictures to help them with the story.

Spend the last couple of minutes asking your child about what they have read. You will find a few examples of questions at the bottom of some pages.

Understanding what they have read is as important as the reading itself.

$O$nce upon a time there was a little girl called Cinderella, who lived with her stepmother and her two stepsisters.

How many stepsisters did Cinderella have?

Cinderella was very pretty and her stepsisters were ugly and nasty.

Poor Cinderella was made to do all the washing, cooking and cleaning around the house.

One day an invitation arrived from the palace for a grand ball and the ugly stepsisters were very excited.

Cinderella asked her stepsisters if she could go.

"You cannot go, look at your old clothes!" they laughed.

Poor Cinderella ran away in tears.

Why couldn't Cinderella go to the ball?

On the night of the ball, after her ugly stepsisters had gone, Cinderella sat beside the fire feeling very sad.

Suddenly, a beautiful fairy appeared beside her.

"I am your Fairy Godmother, and you shall go to the ball!" she said.

Cinderella was so happy.

The Fairy Godmother asked Cinderella to bring her a big pumpkin, two small mice and a lizard.

Then, with one wave of her magic wand, the Fairy Godmother changed the pumpkin into a silver carriage, the mice into white horses and the lizard into a driver.

What did the mice turn into?

"Now we must find you something to wear," said the Fairy Godmother, and she waved her wand again.

Cinderella was now wearing the most beautiful dress she had ever seen.

"Now, off you go to the ball and remember that when the clock strikes midnight, the magic will disappear," said the Fairy Godmother.

"I promise I will remember," said Cinderella.

Cinderella looked so beautiful.

When she arrived at the ball, the Prince saw her and from that moment he could not take his eyes off her.

He asked her to dance and they danced all night long.

Everyone wanted to know who she was and even her two ugly stepsisters did not know.

Suddenly, the clock struck midnight.

Cinderella remembered the Fairy Godmother's words.

What did Cinderella have to remember?

"I have to go!" Cinderella said to the Prince and turned and left as quickly as she could.

As she ran down the stairs, she lost one of her glass shoes.

Her beautiful dress had changed back into her old clothes and the carriage was a pumpkin once more.

What has Cinderella dropped?

Cinderella ran home quickly.

"Where did she go?" asked the Prince.

Many other ladies wanted to dance with him, but he refused.

He wanted Cinderella.

The next day the two ugly stepsisters were very angry because the Prince had not danced with them.

They shouted at Cinderella and ordered her to do her work.

The Prince had found Cinderella's glass shoe on the stairs.

He had fallen in love with her.

He decided that the very next day he would use the glass shoe to find out who she was.

How will he use the glass shoe to find Cinderella?

The Prince went from house to house asking every lady to try the glass shoe on.

Each one tried to squeeze her foot in, but the shoe was just too small!

At last the Prince came to Cinderella's house.

Her two ugly stepsisters grabbed the glass shoe and tried it on.

Their feet were too big.

Why did the glass shoe not fit the ugly stepsisters?

Just then Cinderella came in from the kitchen and asked "Please can I try the shoe on?"

"You?" laughed her ugly stepsisters.

"You were not at the ball, so go back to the kitchen where you belong."

"Let her try," said the Prince.

Cinderella smiled and she sat down beside him.

The shoe fitted perfectly.

The Prince was so happy.

He asked Cinderella to marry him and she said that she would.

The two ugly stepsisters could not believe it.

Soon the Prince and his beautiful Princess were married.

They lived happily ever after.